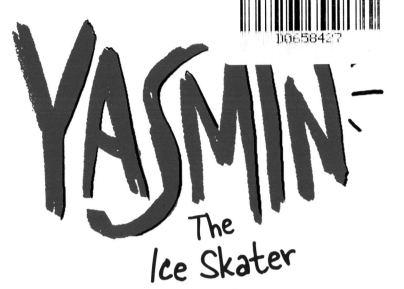

YASMIN

The
Ice Skater

written by
SAADIA FARUQI

illustrated by
HATEM ALY

PICTURE WINDOW BOOKS
a capstone imprint

To Mariam for inspiring me, and Mubashir
for helping me find the right words—S.F.

To my sister, Eman, and her amazing girls,
Jana and Kenzi—H.A.

Yasmin is published by Picture Window Books, an imprint of Capstone.
1710 Roe Crest Drive
North Mankato, Minnesota 56003
capstonepub.com

Text copyright © 2023 by Saadia Faruqi.
Illustrations copyright © 2023 by Capstone.

Library of Congress Cataloging-in-Publication Data
Names: Faruqi, Saadia, author. | Aly, Hatem, illustrator. | Faruqi, Saadia.
Yasmin.
Title: Yasmin the ice skater / written by Saadia Faruqi ; illustrated by
Hatem Aly.
Description: North Mankato, Minnesota : Picture Window Books, [2022]. |
Series: Yasmin | Audience: Ages 5-8. | Audience: Grades K-1. | Summary:
Yasmin and her friend Emma are going to the ice rink, but Yasmin is
nervous and does not want to admit that she has never skated, so she
delays going on the ice as long as possible—but when she falls down
Emma's mother offers to teach her, and Emma helps.
Identifiers: LCCN 2021970061 (print) | LCCN 2021970062 (ebook) |
ISBN 9781663959324 (hardcover) | ISBN 9781666331479 (paperback) |
ISBN 9781666331486 (pdf)
Subjects: LCSH: Muslim girls—Juvenile fiction. | Pakistani Americans—
Juvenile fiction. | Skating—Juvenile fiction. | Embarrassment—Juvenile
fiction. | Friendship—Juvenile fiction. | CYAC: Ice skating—Fiction. |
Embarrassment—Fiction. | Friendship—Fiction. | Muslims—United States—
Fiction. | Pakistani Americans—Fiction.
Classification: LCC PZ7.1.F373 Ygi 2022 (print) | LCC PZ7.1.F373 (ebook)
| DDC [E]—dc23
LC record available at https://lccn.loc.gov/2021970061
LC ebook record available at https://lccn.loc.gov/2021970062

Designer: Kay Fraser

Design Elements: Shutterstock/LiukasArt

TABLE OF CONTENTS

CHAPTER ONE

A New Activity

One Saturday, Yasmin went
on a playdate with Emma.

"Guess where we're going?"
Emma's mother asked the girls.

Yasmin loved guessing games.

"Go-karting?" Yasmin asked.
She liked to go fast!

"Or the trampoline park?"

She liked to jump high!

Mrs. Winters laughed. "Good

guesses, but this is better," she

said. "We're going ice skating!"

Yasmin's stomach filled with bubbles. She'd never skated before. Skating on ice sounded dangerous.

"Great!" Yasmin said, trying to smile.

She didn't want Emma to know she was scared.

Soon, they came to a big building. It was cold inside. Lots of happy families were skating around the rink. They made it look so easy.

Mrs. Winters bought tickets and rented skates. The skates were heavy, and they had sharp blades on the bottom.

Yasmin gulped. How could she tell Emma she was scared to try skating?

CHAPTER TWO

The Ice Rink

Mrs. Winters helped the girls put on their skates. Then they all held hands as they walked toward the ice.

"Let's go skate!" Emma squealed with excitement.

"Can I get a drink of water first?" Yasmin asked.

"Of course," Mrs. Winters said. She passed Yasmin a water bottle from her bag.

Yasmin drank as slowly as she could.

Then they headed toward the
rink once more. They passed a
concession stand. "How about
some snacks?" Yasmin asked.

"We'll get popcorn later," Mrs. Winters said.

At the edge of the rink, Mrs. Winters stopped to talk to a friend.

Emma stepped onto the ice and started skating. "Come on, Yasmin!" she shouted.

Yasmin saw a big screen on the wall. Her favorite cartoon was playing. "I'll be right there!" she shouted back.

While Emma skated loops around the rink, Yasmin watched the cartoon. Too soon, it ended. Finally, Yasmin knew she had to step onto the ice.

Her feet went forward, and the rest of her went backward.

Crash!

Oh no! Now everyone would know she'd never skated before.

⇟ CHAPTER THREE ⇞

Learning to Skate

Mrs. Winters came rushing over.

"I don't know how to skate!" Yasmin said miserably.

"It's okay, dear," Mrs. Winters replied, helping her up. "I'll teach you."

She showed Yasmin how to walk safely on the ice. This was called marching.

Then she showed Yasmin how to glide. "Slow and steady," Mrs. Winters said.

When Yasmin fell down, Mrs. Winters showed her how to get up using her hands and knees. Emma skated over to them. "Want to skate with me, Yasmin?" she asked.

Yasmin wasn't sure she was ready, but she nodded. She didn't want to let Emma down. They held hands tightly and skated slowly around the rink.

"You're doing great, Yasmin!"
Emma said.

They skated together in time
to the music. Everyone looked
like they were having fun. And
so was Yasmin!

The music stopped, and Mrs.

Winters waved to them. "Time to

go, kids!" she called.

"But I just got started!" Yasmin said as they took off their skates.

Emma laughed. "You spent too much time doing other things, silly."

Mrs. Winters laughed too. "Shall we come back next week?" she asked.

Yasmin nodded. "Yes, please!" she said. Then she pointed to the concession stand. "How about that popcorn now?"

Think About It, Talk About It

* Yasmin was nervous about ice skating because she had never tried it before. Do you like to try new things? How do you feel when you try something new?

* Mrs. Winters and Emma helped Yasmin learn to ice skate. Has a family member or relative helped you learn an activity? How is someone teaching you an activity different than teaching yourself?

* Although Yasmin falls while ice skating, she keeps trying. How might the story be different if Yasmin gave up trying?

* Imagine you are teaching a newbie how to do your favorite activity. What are some tips you would give them? Are there any safety tips? Make a list of your tips and advice.

Learn Urdu with Yasmin!

Yasmin's family speaks both English and Urdu. Urdu is a language from Pakistan. Maybe you already know some Urdu words!

baba (BAH-bah)—father

hijab (HEE-jahb)—scarf covering the hair

jaan (jahn)—life; a sweet nickname for a loved one

kameez (kuh-MEEZ)—long tunic or shirt

kitaab (keh-TAB)—book

lassi (LAH-see)—a yogurt drink

nana (NAH-nah)—grandfather on mother's side

nani (NAH-nee)—grandmother on mother's side

salaam (sah-LAHM)—hello

shukriya (shuh-KREE-yuh)—thank you

Pakistan Fun Facts

Yasmin and her family are proud of their Pakistani culture. Yasmin loves to share facts about Pakistan!

Pakistan is on the continent of Asia, with India on one side and Afghanistan on the other.

Islamabad

PAKISTAN

The word Pakistan means "land of the pure" in Urdu and Persian.

Many languages are spoken in Pakistan, including Urdu, English, Saraiki, Punjabi, Pashto, Sindhi, and Balochi.

Mallak Zafar is the first figure skating champion from Pakistan. She began training when she was just five years old!

Field hockey is the official sport of Pakistan. Pakistan has won three gold medals in field hockey at the Olympics.

Make Ice Paint!

SUPPLIES:

- tap water
- ice cube tray
- various colors of food coloring
- craft sticks
- paper to paint on
- newspaper

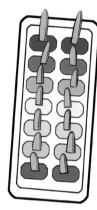

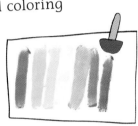

STEPS:

1. Fill the ice cube tray with water.

2. Add a drop of red food coloring to one section and stir with a craft stick. Do this in each section, using a new color and stick each time.

3. You can also mix and match drops of food coloring in the other sections to make new colors. A drop of red and a drop of blue together will make purple. Yellow and red will make orange.

4. Place a craft stick into the middle of each ice cube mold.

5. Freeze at least 4–6 hours.

6. Lay down newspaper under the painting paper.

7. Pull on the craft sticks to remove them from the ice cube tray and use them to paint a picture!

Saadia Faruqi is a Pakistani American writer, interfaith activist, and cultural sensitivity trainer featured in *O, The Oprah Magazine*. She also writes middle grade novels, such as *Yusuf Azeem Is Not A Hero*, and other books for children. Saadia is editor-in-chief of *Blue Minaret*, an online magazine of poetry, short stories, and art. Besides writing books, she also loves reading, binge-watching her favorite shows, and taking naps. She lives in Houston, Texas, with her family.

Hatem Aly is an Egyptian-born illustrator whose work has been featured in multiple publications worldwide. He currently lives in beautiful New Brunswick, Canada, with his wife, son, and more pets than people. When he is not dipping cookies in a cup of tea or staring at blank pieces of paper, he is usually drawing books. One of the books he illustrated is *The Inquisitor's Tale* by Adam Gidwitz, which won a Newbery Honor and other awards, despite Hatem's drawings of a farting dragon, a two-headed cat, and stinky cheese.

Join Yasmin
on all her adventures!

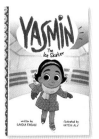

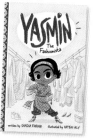